THIS BOOK BELONGS TO...

Name:	Age:

Favourite player:

2022/2023

My Predictions...	Actual...

The Clarets' final position:

The Clarets' top scorer:

Sky Bet Championship winners:

Sky Bet Championship top scorer:

FA Cup winners:

EFL Cup winners:

Contributors: Peter Rogers, Andy Greeves

A TWOCAN PUBLICATION

©2022. Published by twocan under licence from Burnley Football Club.

ISBN: 978-1-914588-64-8

£10

CONTENTS

Once the 2022 FIFA World Cup finals in Qatar are finalised the Clarets will be straight back into the cut and thrust of Championship action. The calendar year of 2023 certainly has some exciting and challenging fixtures on the agenda. Here are six big games for Burnley in 2023.

NEW YEAR SIX PACK

WEST BROMWICH ALBION
HOME · 21 JANUARY 2023

An exciting fixture in the opening weeks of the New Year will see Steve Bruce's West Bromwich Albion visit Turf Moor on 21 January 2023.

Albion has gained a reputation as yo-yo club due to their consistent fleeting between the Championship and Premier League. Just like the Clarets, Albion will have promotion ambitions this season and this mid-winter meeting has all the makings of a Championship classic.

NORWICH CITY
AWAY · 4 FEBRUARY 2023

Burnley and Norwich City locked horns as Premier League rivals last season. Both teams will hope to be right in the promotion mix when the Clarets make the long trip to Norfolk in February.

Despite a disappointing result at Carrow Road last season, the Clarets will be looking for a repeat performance of the 2-0 victory they achieved at Norwich in 2019/20 as they recorded a Premier League double over the Canaries.

WATFORD
HOME · 14 FEBRUARY 2023

The Clarets will find themselves up against another former Premier League club when Watford provide the Valentine's Day opposition here at Turf Moor.

Having suffered a narrow 1-0 defeat away to the Hornets earlier in the 2022/23 campaign, Vincent Kompany's men are sure to be keen to set the record straight against the Hornets on home soil. A Premier League fixture last season, this looks set to be another mouth-watering match at Turf Moor.

BLACKBURN ROVERS
AWAY · 18 MARCH 2023

Burnley make the short trip into enemy territory in mid-March when they face bitter-rivals Blackburn Rovers at Ewood Park in the East Lancashire derby.

The two rivals have not met in a league fixture since the 2015/16 season. After a Scott Arfield goal gave the Clarets local bragging rights with a 1-0 win at Ewood Park - the Clarets then won the home game later in the season to complete a memorable league double en route to promotion and the 2015/16 Championship title.

MIDDLESBROUGH
AWAY · 7 APRIL 2023

The Clarets begin the busy Easter period with a trip to face Middlesbrough at the Riverside Stadium on Good Friday. Burnley knocked Boro out of the FA Cup at the Riverside in January 2016 and our last league victory on Teesside came two years earlier in January 2014.

On that occasion it was current Clarets' forward Jay Rodriguez who opened the scoring after just six minutes in a 2-0 Burnley win.

SHEFFIELD UNITED
HOME · 10 APRIL 2023

Early season pacesetters Sheffield United will travel to Turf Moor in April 2023 as the 2022/23 campaign enters its home straight.

Ben Mee was on target as Burnley recorded a 1-0 Premier League victory over the Blades when the Bramall Lane club last made a visit to Turf Moor. Meanwhile, the last time the two sides met as Championship rivals at Turf Moor was on New Year's Day 2011 when Burnley thumped the visitors 4-2 with goals from Chris Eagles, Chris Iwelumo, Jay Rodriguez and Steven Thompson.

NUMBER OF SEASONS WITH THE CLARETS:

7

BURNLEY LEAGUE APPEARANCES:

282

BURNLEY LEAGUE GOALS:

72

PLAYER OF THE SEASON WINNER:

2003/04

LEGEND V

ROBBIE BLAKE

BURNLEY ACHIEVEMENTS:

Championship Play-Off winners 2008/09

MAJOR STRENGTH: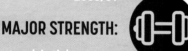

Great footwork in tight spaces, and a ball-playing attacker

INTERNATIONAL ACTION:

Blake never featured in the national colours despite impressive scoring runs at different clubs throughout his career

FINEST HOUR:

Scoring Burnley's first-ever Premier League goal, which also proved to be the winner against Manchester United in an August 2009 clash at Turf Moor

Robbie Blake and Sam Vokes have both been fine servants to Burnley FC, leading the line impressively.

Two years after leaving Burnley, Blake returned for another three years through his love for the club while Welsh international Vokes' Burnley career came in a single seven-year period.

...But which Clarets legend was better?

Defending is not just about stopping the attackers and clearing your lines. Making the best of possession you have just won is vital - although the danger has to be cleared, it is important for your team to keep hold of the ball.

SOCCER SKILLS
LONG PASSES

When passing your way out of defence, and short, side-foot passes are not possible, the longer pass, driven over the heads of midfield players, can be used.

EXERCISE

In an area 40m x 10m, A1 and A2 try to pass accurately to each other, with a defender B, in the middle between them. Player B must attempt to stop the pass if possible, and A1 and A2, must keep the ball within the area of the grids.

After each successful long pass, the end player will exchange a shorter pass with B before passing long again, thus keeping the exercise realistic and also keeping the defender in the middle involved. The player in the middle should be changed every few minutes, and a 'count' of successful passes made for each player.

KEY FACTORS

1   Approach at an angle.
2   Non-kicking foot placed next to the ball.
3   Eye on the ball.
4   Strike underneath the ball & follow through.

Practice is the key to striking a consistently accurate long pass and to developing the timing and power required.

The same end result could be achieved by bending the pass around the defender instead of over him, and this pass could be practised in the same exercise, by striking the football on its outer edge (instead of underneath) which will impart the spin required to make the ball 'bend' around the defender - not an easy skill!

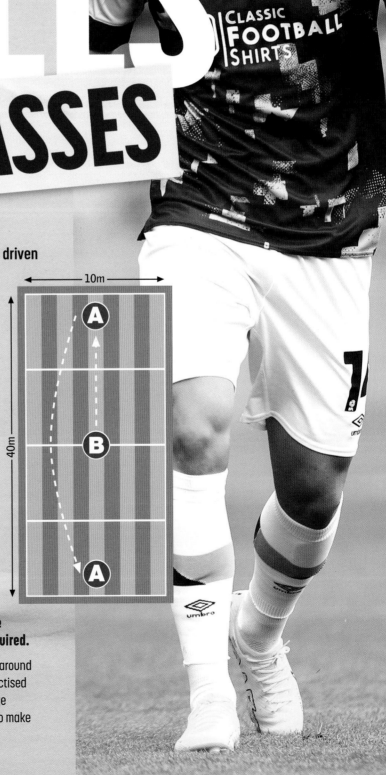

CHAMPIONSHIP
2022/2023
SQUAD

2 MATTHEW LOWTON

DEFENDER   DOB: 09/06/1989   BIRTHPLACE: ENGLAND

A consistent and reliable performer in the Burnley defence, Matt Lowton has amassed over 200 appearances in claret and blue following his June 2015 transfer from Aston Villa.

The 33-year-old brings a wealth of experience to the Clarets' squad and made his first appearance for Vincent Kompany in the League Cup victory over Shrewsbury Town in August 2022.

3 CHARLIE TAYLOR

DEFENDER   DOB: 18/09/1993   BIRTHPLACE: ENGLAND

Recruited from Leeds United in the summer of 2017, Charlie Taylor has established himself as a regular face in the Clarets' starting line-up.

The 29-year-old defender loves to venture forward and support the attack when the opportunity allows, he is now in his sixth season at Turf Moor and has made over 150 senior appearances for the club.

4 JACK CORK

MIDFIELDER   DOB: 25/06/1989   BIRTHPLACE: ENGLAND

Along with Burney teammate Jay Rodriguez, 33-year-old midfielder Jack Cork is also enjoying his second spell at Turf Moor.

A reliable performer, Cork played on loan for the Clarets as a Chelsea player earlier in his career. He returned to the club in the summer of 2017 when he joined permanently from Swansea City. His early Burnley form was rewarded with a full England cap in November 2017.

5 TAYLOR HARWOOD-BELLIS

DEFENDER   DOB: 30/01/2002   BIRTHPLACE: ENGLAND

Burnley were delighted to secure the services of England U21 central defender Taylor Harwood-Bellis in the summer of 2022 when he agreed a season-long loan at Turf Moor from reigning Premier League champions Manchester City.

The Stockport-born defender progressed from the City Academy to Pep Guardiola's first team and has continued his development with a number of loan moves. He has previously worked with Burnley manager Vincent Kompany while at City and also during a loan spell at Anderlecht.

6 CJ EGAN-RILEY

DEFENDER   DOB: 02/01/2003   BIRTHPLACE: ENGLAND

The Clarets captured the signing of versatile defender CJ Egan-Riley from Manchester City on a three-year deal in July 2022. Still only 19, Egan-Riley emerged from the City Academy to make first-team appearances for Pep Guardiola's side in the Premier League, UEFA Champions League and League Cup.

With the flexibility to operate as a central defender, right-back or even as a holding midfield player, Egan-Riley looks set to become a valuable member of the Burnley squad for many seasons to come.

7 JOHANN GUDMUNDSSON

MIDFIELDER DOB: 27/10/1990 BIRTHPLACE: ICELAND

Icelandic international midfielder Johann Gudmundsson has now racked up over 150 Burnley appearances following his arrival at the club in the summer of 2016.

Signed from Charlton Athletic following the Clarets' promotion to the Premier League, Gudmundsson has netted nine goals in Burnley colours as at the start of the 2022/23 Championship campaign. Capped on over 80 occasions by Iceland, his first league outing for Burnley in 2022/23 came in the 5-1 victory at Wigan Athletic in August.

15

8 JOSH BROWNHILL

MIDFIELDER   DOB: 19/12/1995   BIRTHPLACE: ENGLAND

Attacking midfielder Josh Brownhill began life under the management of new boss Vincent Kompany in great form. The former Bristol City man scored four Championship goals in the opening month of the season including a brace in the 5-1 victory away to Wigan.

With the ability to play in a central midfield berth or on the right of midfield, Brownhill looks set to have a major role to play in Kompany's 2022/23 plans.

9 JAY RODRIGUEZ

FORWARD DOB: 29/07/1989 BIRTHPLACE: ENGLAND

Burnley-born Jay Rodriguez is currently enjoying a second spell at the club having returned to Turf Moor in the summer of 2019 following successful spells with Southampton and West Bromwich Albion.

On target with three goals in the opening month of the current campaign, Rodriguez's experience and goals should prove vital to the Clarets across their 2022/23 Championship campaign.

10 ASHLEY BARNES

FORWARD DOB: 30/10/1989 BIRTHPLACE: ENGLAND

Popular striker Ashley Barnes began his tenth season at Turf Moor in the summer of 2022/23 needing just three goals to hit the half century mark of goals for the club.

An all-action forward player who never gives defenders a second of peace, 32-year-old Barnes has a great understanding with fellow forward Jay Rodriguez and is expected to be right among the goals as usual during the current campaign.

11 SCOTT TWINE

FORWARD   DOB: 14/07/1999   BIRTHPLACE: ENGLAND

After starring for MK Dons in their 2021/22 League One campaign, Scott Twine became one of the most wanted players outside of the Premier League. Burnley fended off interest from a host of clubs to land the exciting 22-year-old forward in June 2022.

A fantastic talent from dead ball situations, Twine is more than capable of netting spectacular goals from range. He agreed a four-year deal at Turf Moor and is seen as a key part in the club's aim to return to the Premier League.

14 CONNOR ROBERTS

DEFENDER   DOB: 23/09/1995   BIRTHPLACE: WALES

Maintaining his club form over the first half of the 2022/23 season will be vital for Clarets' right-back Connor Roberts who harbours great hopes of heading to the FIFA World Cup finals in Qatar at the end of 2022 with Wales.

Signed from Swansea City at the start of last season, the attacking right-back made a great impression on the Turf Moor faithful despite the club's relegation from the Premier League.

CHAMPIONSHIP
2022/2023
SQUAD

17 MANUEL BENSON

FORWARD DOB: 28/03/1997 BIRTHPLACE: BELGIUM

Attacking wide-man Manuel Benson forms part of a new-look Burnley squad for 2022/23 having joined the Clarets from Royal Antwerp in August.

On loan at PEC Zwolle last season, Benson clearly impressed Vincent Kompany when playing against his Anderlecht team and the new Burnley boss wasted little time in bringing him to Turf Moor. Benson made his Clarets' debut in the opening home game of the season against Luton Town.

15 BAILEY PEACOCK-FARRELL

GOALKEEPER DOB: 29/10/1996 BIRTHPLACE: N IRELAND

Northern Ireland international goalkeeper Bailey Peacock-Farrell joined the Clarets from Leeds United in August 2019. With Joe Hart and Nick Pope as competition for the No1 sport at Turf Moor at the time, the Darlington-born stopper found first-team opportunities hard to come by.

He enjoyed a valuable loan spell with Sheffield Wednesday last season and having returned to Turf Moor he will provide both cover and competition to Arijanet Muric in 2022/23.

18 ASHLEY WESTWOOD

MIDFIELDER DOB: 01/04/1990 BIRTHPLACE: ENGLAND

A regular face in the Clarets' midfield ever since he joined the club from Aston Villa in 2017, Ashley Westwood featured in 25 Premier League matches last season as Burnley battled for their top-flight status.

He suffered an ankle injury in the 1-1 draw away to West Ham United in April 2022 and is expected to be sidelined until around October. Westwood's return to fitness will certainly be a huge boost to Vincent Kompany's squad.

19 ANASS ZAROURY

FORWARD DOB: 07/11/2000 BIRTHPLACE: BELGIUM

In what was a hectic summer of squad rebuilding at Turf Moor, Belgian U21 international winger Anass Zaroury became the club's 14th new recruit when he joined from Charleroi on 30 August 2022.

A tricky winger with great pace and immaculate close control, Zaroury is a great creator of chances for others but certainly enjoys weighing in with goals of his own too. He agreed a four-year stay at Turf Moor as Burnley continue to reshape the playing squad for an exciting new era at the club.

21 LUKE McNALLY

DEFENDER DOB: 20/09/1999 BIRTHPLACE: ROI

Towering central defender Luke McNally joined the Clarets from Oxford United when he agreed a four-year deal at Turf Moor in June 2022. Capped by the Republic of Ireland at U19 level, McNally's performances at the Kassam Stadium last season won him many admirers.

With big boots to fill in the Clarets' defence following the departures of Ben Mee and James Tarkowski, the 2022/23 season offers 23-year-old McNally the chance to shine at Championship level.

20 DENIS FRANCHI

GOALKEEPER DOB: 22/10/2002 BIRTHPLACE: ITALY

Goalkeeper Denis Franchi joined Burnley from French giants Paris Saint Germain in August 2022, signing a three-year deal.

An Italian U20 international, Franchi has benefitted from training alongside goalkeepers Keylor Navas and fellow Italian Gianluigi Donnarumma at his former club and was named on the first-team bench seven times in all competitions including away at Manchester City in the UEFA Champions League last season.

22 | VITINHO

MIDFIELDER   DOB: 23/07/1999   BIRTHPLACE: BRAZIL

Brazilian Vitinho, whose full name is Victor Alexander da Silva, joined Burnley in July 2022 from Belgian club Cercle Brugge. He agreed a four-year deal at Turf Moor and has the ability to operate at right-back or in a more advanced position on the right side of midfielder where his blistering pace is a real threat.

A regular face in the Burnley team across the opening weeks of the new season, Vitinho netted his first goal for the club in the 2-0 Turf Moor victory over Millwall.

23 | NATHAN TELLA

MIDFIELDER   DOB: 07/07/1999   BIRTHPLACE: ENGLAND

Attacking midfielder Nathan Tella is another promising young talent from the Premier League who has agreed a season-long loan deal at Turf Moor with a view to securing valuable first-team action.

The 23-year-old Southampton Academy graduate will spend the 2022/23 season under the watchful eye of Vincent Kompany and his coaching staff. Tella made a sensational start to his Clarets' career with two goals in the thrilling 3-3 draw with Blackpool at Turf Moor on 20 August before then adding his name to the scoresheet a week later with the Clarets' third goal in the 5-1 win at Wigan Athletic.

24 JOSH CULLEN

MIDFIELDER DOB: 07/04/1996 BIRTHPLACE: ROI

Midfielder Josh Cullen followed Vincent Kompany from Anderlecht to Turf Moor in the summer of 2022. A current Republic of Ireland international, Cullen began his career with West Ham United where he cited Hammers' legend Mark Noble as having a great influence on his career.

During his time at West Ham he gained great Football League experience with loan spells at Bradford City, Bolton Wanderers and Charlton Athletic before trying his luck in the Belgian game in 2020.

25 WILL NORRIS

GOALKEEPER DOB: 12/08/1993 BIRTHPLACE: ENGLAND

The Clarets strengthened the club's goalkeeping ranks with the signing of 29-year-old stopper Will Norris from Wolverhampton Wanderers in August 2020.

Norris made his debut in the FA Cup third round match with MK Dons in January 2021 when his penalty saves helped the Clarets progress to round four following a 4-3 shoot-out success. He also played in the club's final two Premier League games when Nick Pope was sidelined through injury.

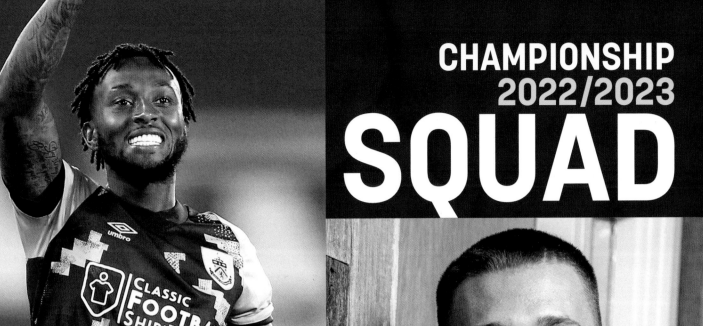

26 SAMUEL BASTIEN

MIDFIELDER DOB: 26/09/1996 BIRTHPLACE: DR CONGO

Midfielder Samuel Bastien joined Vincent Kompany's Burnley revolution in the summer of 2022 when he made the switch from Standard Liege and agreed a three-year deal at Turf Moor.

Capped on seven occasions by the DR Congo national team, Bastien has swiftly settled into his new surroundings with a string of impressive performances for Burnley and was on target in the EFL Cup victory over Shrewsbury and the 5-2 demolition of Wigan Athletic in the Championship.

27 DARKO CHURLINOV

FORWARD DOB: 11/07/2000 BIRTHPLACE: NORTH MACEDONIA

A North Macedonian international forward, Darko Churlinov joined the Clarets in August 2022 from German cub VfB Stuttgart. Amazingly the 22-year-old holds the record of being the youngest player to have represented Macedonia's national team having been aged just 16 years and eight months when he made his international debut.

Churlinov's first appearance for Burnley came less than 24 hours after signing when he came off the bench at Turf Moor against Blackpool, while his full debut came in the EFL Cup win at Shrewsbury Town a few days later.

28 KEVIN LONG

DEFENDER   DOB: 18/08/1990   BIRTHPLACE: ROI

Long-serving defender Kevin Long featured in six Premier League fixtures last season as Burnley fought against relegation. The former Republic of Ireland international has previously experienced relegation and promotion as a Burnley player and will therefore know better than most what is needed for the club to succeed in 2022/23.

With a host of young defenders joining the club's ranks in the summer of 2022, Long's vast knowledge of the game is sure to be a great benefit to those around him.

29 IAN MAATSEN

DEFENDER   DOB: 10/02/2002   BIRTHPLACE: NETHERLANDS

Highly-rated left-back Ian Maatsen is on a season-long loan with the Clarets from Premier League Chelsea. A Netherlands U21 international, Maatsen arrived at Turf Moor with valuable Championship experience already under his belt having spent last season with Coventry City where his performances on loan for the Sky Blues won him rave reviews.

The 20-year-old defender wasted little time in impressing his new fans as he netted the Clarets' first goal of the new season to secure a 1-0 win away to Huddersfield Town.

CHAMPIONSHIP
2022/2023
SQUAD

30 HALIL DERVISOGLU

FORWARD DOB: 08/12/1999 BIRTHPLACE: TURKEY

Halil Dervişoğlu joined Burnley on deadline day of the summer transfer window in September 2022, when the 22-year-old agreed a season-long loan from Brentford.

Having joined the Bees in 2020 from Sparta Rotterdam, Dervişoğlu has since gained valuable experience with previous loan spells at FC Twente and Galatasaray. Highly regarded by Turkey at international level, Dervişoğlu has won 13 caps and scored six goals at the time of his arrival at Turf Moor.

36 JORDAN BEYER

DEFENDER DOB: 19/05/2000 BIRTHPLACE: GERMANY

Burnley secured the season-long loan signing of defender Jordan Beyer from Bundesliga side Borussia Mönchengladbach on the final day of the 2022 summer transfer window.

The 22-year-old, who can operate as a centre-back and a right-back, leaves Mönchengladbach for the 2022/23 campaign, where he has spent the last seven seasons, after joining the club as an U16 player in 2015.

49 ARIJANET MURIC

GOALKEEPER DOB: 07/11/1998 BIRTHPLACE: KOSOVO

Giant goalkeeper Arijanet Muric became new boss Vincent Kompany's eighth summer signing when he reunited with his former Manchester City teammate. Muric joined City back in 2015, where he was a part of the first-team squad for two years, with Kompany as captain.

Internationally, the 23-year-old represented Montenegro at U21 level, before switching allegiances to Kosovo in 2018, with 27 senior appearances now to his name. He marked his Clarets' debut with a clean sheet as Burnley won 1-0 at Huddersfield Town on opening night. His first Turf Moor shut-out came in the 2-0 victory over Millwall.

MULTIPLE CHOICE

Here are ten Multiple Choice questions to challenge your footy knowledge!

Good luck...

ANSWERS ON PAGE 62

1. What was the name of Tottenham Hotspur's former ground?

A) White Rose Park
B) White Foot Way
C) White Hart Lane

2. Which club did Steven Gerrard leave to become Aston Villa manager?

A) Liverpool
B) Glasgow Rangers
C) LA Galaxy

3. Mohamed Salah and Son Heung-min were joint winners of the Premier League Golden Boot as the division's top scorers in 2021/22.

How many goals did they score?

A) 23   B) 24   C) 25

4. What is the nationality of Manchester United boss Erik ten Hag?

A) Swiss   B) Dutch
C) Swedish

5. Where do Everton play their home games?

A) Goodison Road
B) Goodison Way
C) Goodison Park

6. From which club did Arsenal sign goalkeeper Aaron Ramsdale?

A) Sheffield United
B) Stoke City
C) AFC Bournemouth

7. What is Raheem Sterling's middle name?

A) Shaun
B) Shaquille
C) Silver

8. Who won the 2021/22 League One Play-Off final?

A) Wigan Athletic
B) Sunderland
C) Rotherham United

9. At which ground did the Clarets begin their 2022/23 Championship campaign?

A) Carrow Road
B) Loftus Road
C) The John Smith's Stadium

10. From which club did Burnley sign Josh Brownhill in January 2020?

A) Millwall
B) Bristol City
C) Stoke City

6

CJ
EGAN-RILEY

CLASSIC FAN'TASTIC

Bertie Bee is hiding in the crowd in five different places as Burnley fans celebrate promotion to the Premier League in 2016. Can you find all five?

BURNLEY F.C.
CHAMPIONS
2015/16

11

SCOTT
TWINE

30

Close control in tight situations creates havoc in opposition defences - particularly when receiving the ball in the air - and nine times out of ten, when a striker receives the ball, he has his back to goal.

SOCCER SKILLS
RECEIVING THE BALL

Quite often the ball will arrive in the air, and good strikers have to be able to cope with that - controlling and turning in one movement, ready for the instant shot.

EXERCISE 1

In an area 20m x 10m, two players A and A2 test the man in the middle, B, by initially throwing the ball at him in the air, with the instruction to turn and play in to the end man - if possible using only two touches.

The middle player is changed regularly, and to make things more realistic, the end players progress to chipping the ball into the middle.

The middle player is asked to receive and turn using chest, thigh, or instep.

KEY FACTORS

1 Assess flight early - get in position.
2 Cushion the ball.
3 Be half-turned as you receive.

EXERCISE 2

A progression of this exercise is the following, where the ball is chipped or driven in to the striker from varying positions. He has to receive with his back to goal, and using just two touches in total if possible, shoot past the keeper into the goal!

To make this even more difficult, a defender can be brought in eventually. For younger children, the 'servers' should throw the ball to ensure consistent quality.

TRAIN TO WIN

Making sure that you are fit, healthy and fully prepared is key to success in whatever challenge you are taking on. Those three factors are certainly vital for professional footballers and also for any young aspiring player who plays for his or her school or local football team. The importance of fitness, health and preparation are key factors behind the work that goes into preparing the Burnley players to perform at their maximum on matchday.

The Clarets players will need to demonstrate peak levels of fitness if they want to feature in Vincent Kompany's team. Before anyone can think of pulling on a claret and blue shirt and stepping out at Turf Moor, they will have had to perform well at the Training Ground to have shown the manager, his coaches and fitness staff that they are fully fit and ready for the physical challenges that await them on a matchday.

Regardless of whether training takes place at the training ground or at the stadium, the players' fitness remains an all-important factor. Of course time spent practicing training drills and playing small-sided games will help a player's fitness but there is lots of work undertaken just to ensure maximum levels of fitness are reached.

Away from the training pitches the players will spend a great deal of time in the gymnasium partaking in their own personal work-outs. Bikes, treadmills and weights will all form part of helping the players reach and maintain a top level of fitness.

Over the course of a week the players will take part in many warm-up and aerobic sessions and even complete yoga and pilates classes to help with core strength and general fitness. The strength and conditioning coaches at the club work tirelessly to do all they can to make sure that the players you see in action are at their physical peak come kick-off.

While the manager and his staff will select the team and agree the tactics, analysts will provide the players and staff with details on the opposition's strengths, weaknesses and their likely approach to the match.

Suffice to say the training ground is a busy place and no stone is left unturned in preparation for the big match!

NUMBER OF SEASONS WITH THE CLARETS:

6 and a bit!

BURNLEY LEAGUE APPEARANCES:

282

BURNLEY LEAGUE GOALS:

23

PLAYER OF THE SEASON WINNER:

2006/07 & 2007/08

LEGEND

WADE ELLIOTT

BURNLEY ACHIEVEMENTS:

Championship Play-Off winners 2008/09

MAJOR STRENGTH:

Excellent range of passing and the ability to link play

INTERNATIONAL ACTION:

Elliott didn't play international football during his career

FINEST HOUR:

His 25-yard, curling shot that clinched Burnley's promotion to the Premier League as the Clarets beat Sheffield United 1-0 in the Championship Play-Off final of 2009

Two attack-minded midfielders, Wade Elliott and George Boyd were key members of Burnley's promotion-winning sides during their time at Turf Moor.

The pair scored 35 goals between them in the famous claret shirt and memorable efforts include Elliott's Championship Play-Off final winner against Sheffield United in 2009 and a Boyd strike which gave Burnley a victory over Premier League champions Manchester City in 2015.

Both players would bring flair and creativity to any side, but which would the first name on your team sheet?

LEGEND
GEORGE BOYD

**NUMBER OF SEASONS
WITH THE CLARETS:**

3

**BURNLEY
LEAGUE APPEARANCES:**

123

BURNLEY LEAGUE GOALS:

12

PLAYER OF THE SEASON WINNER:

2014/15

BURNLEY ACHIEVEMENTS:

Championship winners
2015/16

INDIVIDUAL ACHIEVEMENTS:

PFA League Two Team of the Year 2007/08
PFA League One Team of the Year 2008/09

INTERNATIONAL ACTION:

Initially capped by England 'C', Boyd switched
his international allegiance in 2009 and went
on represent Scotland at 'B' and senior level.
His two senior Scotland appearances came
against Serbia in 2013 and Nigeria in 2014

FINEST HOUR:

A powerful, left-footed volley from
the edge of the penalty area that
gave Burnley a 1-0 win over reigning
Premier League champions,
Manchester City, in March 2015

DREAM TEAM

Pick your ultimate Burnley
dream team and design them a kit!

9

JAY RODRIGUEZ

CHAMPIONSHIP DANGER MEN

24 STARS TO WATCH OUT FOR DURING 2022/23

BIRMINGHAM CITY

PRZEMYSLAW PLACHETA

A Polish international and true speed merchant, Przemyslaw Placheta is on a season long loan at St Andrew's from Championship rivals Norwich City.

The 24-year-old forward tends to operate on the left side of the Blues' attack and marked his home debut for Birmingham City with a goal in their 2-1 victory over Huddersfield Town in August.

BLACKBURN ROVERS

LEWIS TRAVIS

All-action central midfielder Lewis Travis was at the heart of Blackburn Rovers' impressive 2021/22 Championship campaign featuring in all bar one of the club's league games last season.

With the ability to carry the ball forward and help his team turn defence into attack, 25-year-old Travis has won many admirers for his energetic displays in the Rovers engine room.

BRISTOL CITY

ANDREAS WEIMANN

Austrian international forward Andreas Weimann was the Robins' leading scorer last season with 22 goals in 45 Championship games.

An experienced and proven goalscorer at this level, Weimann, who had scored goals at second tier level for Watford, Derby County and Wolves before moving to Ashton Gate, netted in each of the first three league games of the new 2022/23 season.

BURNLEY

JAY RODRIGUEZ

Now in his second spell at Turf Moor, Burnley-born forward Jay Rodriguez is expected to have a big role to play for the Clarets in 2022/23 as the club looks to bounce back to the Premier League at the first attempt.

A former England international, Rodriguez played top-flight football for Southampton and WBA before rejoining the Clarets in 2019.

BLACKPOOL

THEO CORBEANU

Blackpool signed Canadian international forward Theo Corbeanu on a season-long loan from Wolves in July 2022.

Standing at 6ft 3ins, the 20-year-old brings a real presence to the Seasiders' attack and was on target in both of Blackpool's thrilling 3-3 draws against Burnley and Bristol City in August and following the sale of Josh Bowler he could well be the go-to man for goals at Bloomfield Road in 2022/23.

CARDIFF CITY

MAX WATTERS

Exciting striker Max Watters will be looking to cement his place in the Cardiff City attack in 2022/23. After joining the Bluebirds in January 2021 from Crawley, Watters was loaned to League One MK Dons in 2021/22.

However, Cardiff boss Steve Morison has handed Max the chance to make his mark with a series of starts as Cardiff's got the new season underway in impressive form.

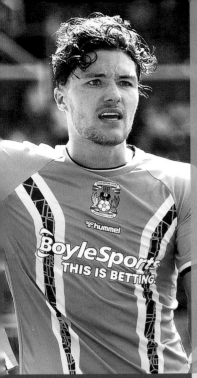

COVENTRY CITY

CALLUM O'HARE

Attacking midfielder Callum O'Hare enjoyed a highly impressive 2021/22 season and has gained the reputation of being both City's star performer and one of the most creative midfielders operating in the Championship.

With fantastic close control and superb awareness of teammates, O'Hare is blessed with great balance when in possession and the eye for a decisive pass.

LUTON TOWN

ELIJAH ADEBAYO

Elijah Adebayo topped the Luton Town scoring charts last season with 16 Championship goals at the Hatters reached the end-of-season Play-Offs.

A strong target man, Adebayo is expected to form an impressive strike partnership at Kenilworth Road this season with Luton new boy Carlton Morris who joined in the summer from Barnsley.

HUDDERSFIELD TOWN

JORDAN RHODES

Striker Jordan Rhodes has netted over 200 career goals since emerging though the Ipswich Town youth system back in 2007.

Now in his second spell with Huddersfield Town, 32-year-old Rhodes scored 87 goals in 148 outings during his first spell at the club. He returned to the Terriers in 2021 and scored the winning goal in last season's Play-Off semi-final against Luton Town.

MIDDLESBROUGH

MATT CROOKS

An all-action attacking midfielder who can also operate as an out-and-out striker, Matt Crooks joined Middlesbrough in the summer of 2021.

Signed on the back of a number of impressive seasons with Rotherham United, Crooks hit double figures in his first season at the Riverside and is sure to play a big part for Chris Wilder's team this time around.

HULL CITY

OSCAR ESTUPINAN

The Tigers completed the signing of Columbian international striker Oscar Estupinan in July 2022.

His arrival created a level of excitement around the MKM Stadium and the Columbian soon showed his capabilities with both goals as Hull pulled off a surprise victory over Norwich City in August 2022. A strong and mobile front man, Estupinan's goals may well help fire the Tigers up the table this season.

MILLWALL

BARTOSZ BIALKOWSKI

Polish international keeper Bartosz Bialkowski has been ever present in the Lions' last two Championship campaigns.

The 6ft 4in stopper is widely regarded as one of the most reliable goalkeepers in the division. Blessed with excellent reflexes, Bialkowski is an intimidating opponent in one-on-one situations and his command of the penalty area certainly provides great confidence for those operating in front of him

NORWICH CITY
TEEMU PUKKI

A Championship title winner on each occasion that he has played at this level, City's Finnish international striker will be searching a hat-trick of promotions from the second tier in 2022/23.

A real threat in and around the penalty area, Pukki netted 29 goals in the Canaries' 2018/19 title-winning campaign and 26 two season later as they went up as champions.

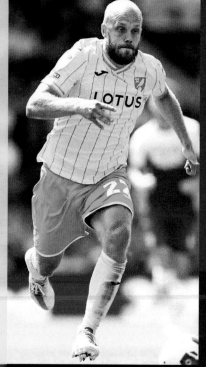

READING
THOMAS INCE

A much-travelled forward, Thomas Ince joined Reading on loan from Stoke City in January 2022 and played a key role him helping the Royals retain their Championship status last season.

Playing under the management of his father, Paul, Ince Jnr then joined Reading on a permanent basis in the summer of 2022. His attacking play and appetite to shoot from distance have won him great popularity with the Reading fans.

ROTHERHAM UNITED
DAN BARLASER

Goalscoring midfielder Dan Barlaser weighed in with nine goals in Rotherham United's League One promotion-winning campaign.

He progressed through the Newcastle United Academy and after gaining valuable experience on loan with the Millers he joined on a permanent basis in October 2020. Seen as the man that makes United tick, a great deal will be expected of the 25-year-old former England youth international in 2022/23.

PRESTON NORTH END
EMIL RIIS JAKOBSEN

Former Denmark U21 international forward Emil Riis Jakobsen enjoyed a highly productive 2021/22 season with Preston North End.

A powerful 6ft 3in frontman, he was the side's standout performer with 20 goals in all competitions last season. The 24-year-old is blessed with great physical strength while also displaying calmness in front of goal.

SHEFFIELD UNITED
OLIVER NORWOOD

Northern Ireland international midfielder Oliver Norwood is something of a Championship promotion-winning specialist.

The 31-year-old has previously won promotion from this division with Brighton, Fulham and as a Sheffield United player in 2018/19. He scored his first goal of the new season as the Blades defeated Blackburn Rovers 3-0 in the opening month of the season.

QUEENS PARK RANGERS
ILIAS CHAIR

The creative spark in the QPR team, Moroccan international Ilias Chair chipped in with nine Championship goals in 2021/22.

A true midfield playmaker, Chair has the ability to open up the tightest of defences and pick out teammates with his exquisite range of passing. The skilful Moroccan is sure to be the man that new Rangers boss Mike Beale looks to build his team around.

STOKE CITY
DWIGHT GAYLE

Much-travelled goal-getter Gayle joined Stoke City from Newcastle United in the summer of 2022.

A nimble front man with the ability to score all manner of goals, his arrival at Stoke was met with great delight. While on loan at WBA in 2018/19 he riffled home an impressive 23 Championship goals and the Potters with be hopeful of a good goal return from their new signing this season.

CHAMPIONSHIP DANGER MEN

24 STARS TO WATCH OUT FOR DURING 2022/23

WATFORD
KEINAN DAVIS

Following an impressive loan spell with Nottingham Forest last season, Aston Villa striker Keinan Davis will be keen to help the Hornets push for an instant return to the Premier League having agreed a season-long loan at Vicarage Road.

Standing at 6ft and 3ins, the 24-year-old striker has pace and power in abundance and is sure to thrill the Watford fans during his loan spell.

SUNDERLAND
ROSS STEWART

On target in SAFC's 2-0 League One Play-Off final victory over Wycombe Wanderers at Wembley, striker Stewart riffled home an impressive 26 goals in all competitions last season.

The Scotland international wasted little time in stepping up to the plate at Championship level as he netted two goals in his first three league games of the new 2022/23 season for the Black Cats.

WEST BROMWICH ALBION
KARLAN GRANT

Former Charlton Athletic and Huddersfield Town striker Karlan Grant scored 18 times in West Bromwich's Albion's 2021/22 Championship campaign.

The 25-year-old appears to be the go to man for goals again in 2022/23 for Steve Bruce's men and has already been on target in the Championship and EFL Cup this season.

SWANSEA CITY
MICHAEL OBAFEMI

A two-goal hero in Swansea City's 4-0 thrashing of South Wales rivals Cardiff City last season, pacy striker Michael Obafemi netted twelve Championship goals for the Swans last season.

Having formed a great understanding with fellow front man Joel Piroe in 2021/22, Swans' boss Russell Martin will have great hopes for Republic of Ireland international Obamfemi again in 2022/23.

WIGAN ATHLETIC
CALLUM LANG

A product of the Wigan Athletic academy, Liverpool-born forward Callum Lang has firmly established himself in the Latics' first team as an attacking player with the ability to create chances for team-mates while also score goals himself.

The 23-year-old was in exceptional form throughout 2021/22 when he made 42 League One appearances and scored 15 as the Latics marched to the title.

2

MATTHEW LOWTON

TRUE OR FALSE?

Here are ten fun footy True or False teasers for you to tackle! Good luck...

ANSWERS ON PAGE 62

2. The FIFA World Cup in 2026 is due to be hosted in the USA, Mexico and Canada

3. Manchester City's former ground was called Maine Park

1. England star Harry Kane has only ever played club football for Spurs

4. Liverpool's Jurgen Klopp has never managed the German national team

5. Gareth Southgate succeeded Roy Hodgson as England manager

6. Manchester United's Old Trafford has the largest capacity in the Premier League

7. Jordan Pickford began his career at Everton

8. Huddersfield Town's nickname is the Terriers

9. Burnley signed Scott Twine from Oxford United

10. Matej Vydra's last Premier League goal for the Clarets came against Wolverhampton Wanderers

43

NUMBER OF SEASONS WITH THE CLARETS:

3

BURNLEY LEAGUE APPEARANCES:

108

BURNLEY LEAGUE GOALS:

7

PLAYER OF THE SEASON WINNER:

Never

LEGEND

MICHAEL KEANE

BURNLEY ACHIEVEMENTS: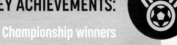

Championship winners 2015/16

MAJOR STRENGTH:

Leaping high to dominate aerially and winning balls both defensively and at the other end of the pitch

INTERNATIONAL ACTION:

Keane has won twelve England caps, scoring once in a 5-1 away victory against Montenegro in 2019

FINEST HOUR:

Scoring his first Premier League goal against Watford in 2016

Michael Keane was a Manchester United academy graduate, while Clarke Carlisle spent his youth days at Blackpool, and dotted around the country throughout his playing career.

Both had excellent stints with Burnley, but who was better?

LEGEND
CLARKE CARLISLE

NUMBER OF SEASONS WITH THE CLARETS:

4

BURNLEY LEAGUE APPEARANCES:

152

BURNLEY LEAGUE GOALS:

9

PLAYER OF THE SEASON WINNER:

Never

BURNLEY ACHIEVEMENTS:

Championship Play-Off winners 2008/09

MAJOR STRENGTH:

Playing out from the back with pinpoint passing to his teammates

INTERNATIONAL ACTION:

Although he played three times for England's U21 team in 2000, Carlisle never played for the senior side

FINEST HOUR:

Winning the Man of the Match award in Burnley's Championship Play-Off final win against Sheffield United in May 2009

CLUB SEARCH

EVERY TEAM OF THE CHAMPIONSHIP IS HIDDEN IN THE GRID, EXCEPT FOR ONE... CAN YOU WORK OUT WHICH ONE?

```
J  B  R  A  L  G  V  N  O  R  W  I  C  H  C  I  T  Y  M  H
A  I  M  O  U  Z  E  K  F  X  R  W  F  U  C  C  D  I  S  W
B  R  I  S  T  O  L  C  I  T  Y  C  B  L  A  E  S  W  P  E
L  M  D  A  O  H  V  E  L  P  D  N  A  L  R  E  D  N  U  S
A  I  D  C  N  B  E  L  W  L  O  Q  I  C  D  W  Y  R  L  T
C  N  L  I  T  U  D  R  E  I  A  V  A  I  I  Q  P  D  O  B
K  G  E  T  O  U  N  U  H  P  U  W  H  T  F  I  T  E  L  R
B  H  S  E  W  H  E  B  N  A  I  O  L  Y  F  M  U  T  S  O
U  A  B  L  N  Y  H  T  V  R  M  J  N  L  C  H  D  I  C  M
R  M  R  H  U  O  T  K  L  N  C  U  S  G  I  J  J  N  Y  W
N  C  O  T  M  A  R  I  Y  O  W  T  N  D  T  M  Q  U  T  I
R  I  U  A  B  U  O  T  C  A  O  I  E  I  Y  U  R  D  I  C
O  T  G  N  U  F  N  S  T  A  D  P  G  M  T  M  X  L  C  H
V  Y  H  A  Y  S  N  F  C  A  E  I  K  A  S  E  M  E  E  A
E  I  G  G  E  G  O  I  E  K  O  S  B  C  S  Y  D  I  K  L
R  A  Q  I  L  R  T  R  P  L  U  E  N  O  A  O  E  F  O  B
S  H  T  W  D  Z  S  F  O  E  G  T  X  A  D  L  R  F  T  I
D  B  U  R  N  L  E  Y  R  A  S  O  A  K  W  I  B  E  S  O
C  O  V  E  N  T  R  Y  C  I  T  Y  R  F  N  S  B  H  Z  N
Q  U  E  E  N  S  P  A  R  K  R  A  N  G  E  R  S  S  A  H
```

Birmingham City	Coventry City	Norwich City	Stoke City
Blackburn Rovers	Huddersfield Town	Preston North End	Sunderland
Blackpool	Hull City	Queens Park Rangers	Swansea City
Bristol City	Luton Town	Reading	Watford
Burnley	Middlesbrough	Rotherham United	West Bromwich Albion
Cardiff City	Millwall	Sheffield United	Wigan Athletic

ANSWERS ON PAGE 62

14

CONNOR ROBERTS

WHICH BALL?

Can you work out which is the actual match ball in these two action pics?

ANSWERS ON PAGE 62

NAME THE SEASON

Can you recall the campaign when these magic moments occurred? **Good luck...**

ANSWERS ON PAGE 62

1. In which season did Chelsea last win the UEFA Champions League?

2. When were Manchester United last Premier League champions?

3. At the end of which season were England crowned World Cup winners?

4. In which season did Aleksandar Mitrovic net 43 Championship goals for Fulham?

5. In which season did Leicester City become Premier League champions?

6. When did Tottenham Hotspur last reach the League Cup final?

7. In which season were Sheffield United last promoted to the Premier League?

8. When did Manchester City win their first Premier League title?

9. During which season did Ashley Barnes join Burnley from Brighton & Hove Albion?

10. In which season did Burnley beat Sheffield United in the Championship Play-Off final?

49

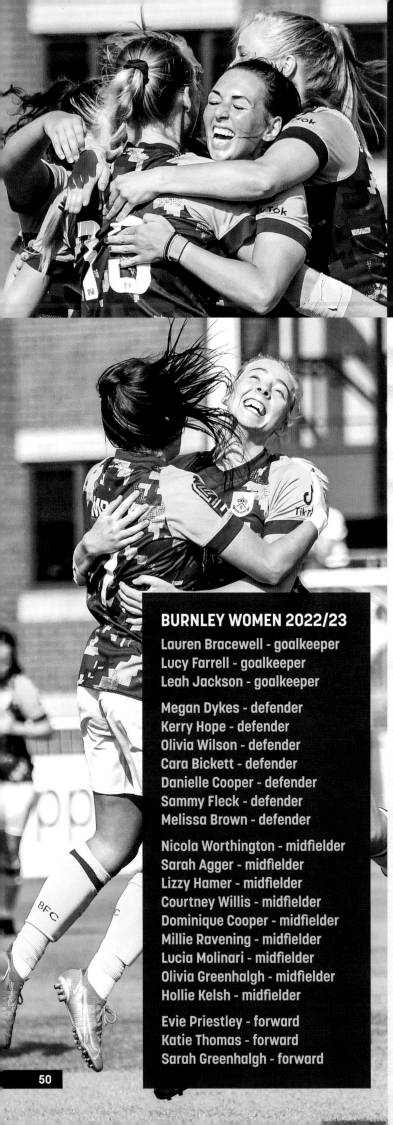

BURNLEY WOMEN

After England's fantastic achievement in winning the woman's UEFA European Championships in the summer of 2022, the profile of girls' and women's football continues to grow and grow.

Ahead of the new 2022/23 season, Burnley's own women's team has welcomed many new faces to the squad for their FA Women's National League North campaign.

The 2022/23 season promises to be the beginning of an exciting new era for Burnley women after it was announced in February 2022 that the women's team would be integrated into Burnley Football Club, as the club's American owner Alan Pace sought to turn the women's team professional.

Highly respected women's coach Jonathan Morgan was appointed as the new head coach of the women's first team in May. Morgan arrives at the club having guided Leicester City women to the Women's Championship title in 2020/21 and into the Women's Super League for the first time in their history.

The team primarily play their home games on a Sunday at Lancashire Football Association's County Ground in Leyland where new supporters are always welcome.

With the interest in the Burnley women's first team on the up, the club continues to work in growing the women's game at all levels while providing a development pathway for young girls to benefit from.

Full details of the Burnley women's team and their 2022/23 fixtures can be found on the club's official website burnleyfootballclub.com

BURNLEY WOMEN 2022/23

Lauren Bracewell - goalkeeper
Lucy Farrell - goalkeeper
Leah Jackson - goalkeeper

Megan Dykes - defender
Kerry Hope - defender
Olivia Wilson - defender
Cara Bickett - defender
Danielle Cooper - defender
Sammy Fleck - defender
Melissa Brown - defender

Nicola Worthington - midfielder
Sarah Agger - midfielder
Lizzy Hamer - midfielder
Courtney Willis - midfielder
Dominique Cooper - midfielder
Millie Ravening - midfielder
Lucia Molinari - midfielder
Olivia Greenhalgh - midfielder
Hollie Kelsh - midfielder

Evie Priestley - forward
Katie Thomas - forward
Sarah Greenhalgh - forward

1. WHO AM I?

2. WHO AM I?

3. WHO AM I?

4. WHO AM I?

ANSWERS ON PAGE 62

WHO ARE YER?

Can you figure out who each of these Clarets stars is?

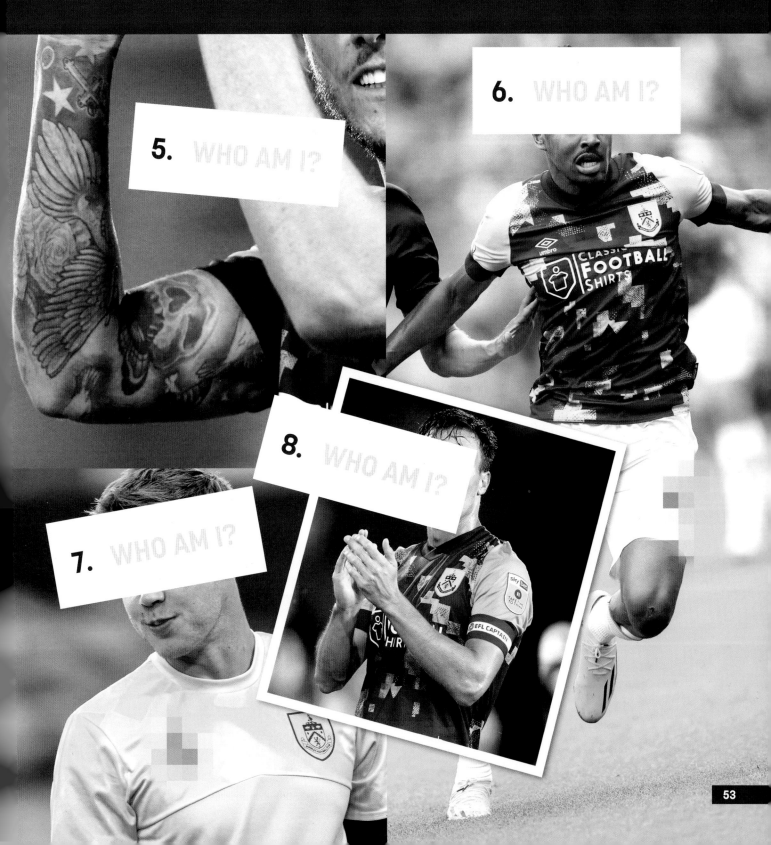

5. WHO AM I?

6. WHO AM I?

7. WHO AM I?

8. WHO AM I?

8

JOSH
BROWNHILL

Can you colour
in this picture
of Josh Brownhill?

TRUE
COLOURS

Burnley

PREMIER LEAGUE CHAMPIONS

Liverpool

FAST FORWARD>>

Do your predictions for 2022/23 match our own?...

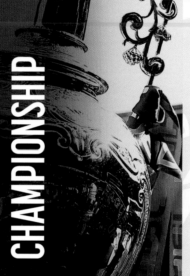

CHAMPIONSHIP

CHAMPIONSHIP RUNNERS-UP

Norwich City

PREMIER LEAGUE

PREMIER LEAGUE RUNNERS-UP

Chelsea

PREMIER LEAGUE TOP SCORER

Erling Haaland

CHAMPIONSHIP TOP SCORER

Ashley Barnes

LEAGUE ONE TOP SCORER
Conor Chaplin

FA CUP WINNERS
Spurs

LEAGUE CUP WINNERS
Leicester City

LEAGUE CUP

LEAGUE ONE CHAMPIONS
Ipswich Town

CHAMPIONS LEAGUE

CHAMPIONS LEAGUE WINNERS
Real Madrid

LEAGUE ONE RUNNERS-UP
Oxford United

LEAGUE ONE

EUROPA LEAGUE WINNERS
Roma

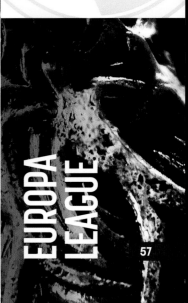

EUROPA LEAGUE

57

NUMBER OF SEASONS WITH THE CLARETS:

6

BURNLEY LEAGUE APPEARANCES:

155

BURNLEY LEAGUE GOALS:

0

PLAYER OF THE SEASON WINNER:

2017/18 & 2019/20

LEGEND

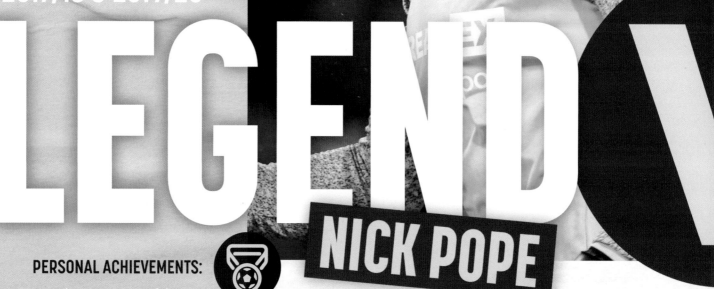

NICK POPE

PERSONAL ACHIEVEMENTS:

PFA Premier League Team of the Year 2019/20

MAJOR STRENGTH:

Close-range shot-stopping and fast reflexes, making himself big

INTERNATIONAL ACTION:

As of August 2022, Pope has played eight times for England under Gareth Southgate and was included in the 2018 World Cup squad before even making his international debut

FINEST HOUR:

Coming second in the race for the Premier League Golden Glove award in 2019/20

After many loan spells, Nick Pope found himself a regular in Burnley's squad in 2016, and has only got better since. Brain Jensen started out in Denmark before settling for ten years in Burnley between 2003 and 2013.

Who has the edge here?

LEGEND

BRIAN JENSEN

NUMBER OF SEASONS WITH THE CLARETS:
10

BURNLEY LEAGUE APPEARANCES:
310

BURNLEY LEAGUE GOALS:
0

PLAYER OF THE SEASON WINNER:
Never

BURNLEY ACHIEVEMENTS:
Championship Play-Offs winners 2008/09

MAJOR STRENGTH:
A perfect frame for a goalkeeper (6ft 5in), Brian excelled in one-on-one situations and making saves at full-stretch

OTHER ACHIEVEMENTS:
NIFL Premiership winners (with Crusaders 2017/18)

FINEST HOUR:
Reaching a landmark of 300 Burnley appearances in a 4-0 victory over Hull City in 2010

59

IDENTIFY THE STAR

Can you put a name to the football stars in these ten teasers?

Good luck...

ANSWERS ON PAGE 62

1. Manchester City's title-winning 'keeper Ederson shared the 2021/22 Golden Glove award for the number of clean sheets with which Premier League rival?

2. Which Portuguese superstar re-joined Manchester United in the 2021/22 season?

3. Can you name the Brazilian forward who joined Aston Villa in May 2022 following a loan spell at Villa Park?

4. Who became Arsenal manager in 2019?

5. Who scored the winning goal in the 2021/22 UEFA Champions League final?

6. After 550 games for West Ham United, which long-serving midfielder announced his retirement in 2022?

7. Who took the mantle of scoring Brentford's first Premier League goal?

8. Who scored the final goal for Manchester City in their 2021/22 Premier League title-winning season?

9. Which Dutch U21 international left-back joined the Clarets on loan for the 2022/23 season from Chelsea?

10. Who was the last Burnley player to play for England?

60

5

TAYLOR
HARWOOD-BELLIS

ANSWERS

PAGE 26 · MULTIPLE CHOICE

1. C. 2. B. 3. A. 4. B. 5. C. 6. A. 7. B. 8. B. 9. C. 10. B.

PAGE 28 · FAN'TASTIC

PAGE 43 · TRUE OR FALSE?

1. False, Harry played on loan for Leyton Orient, Millwall, Norwich City & Leicester City. 2. True. 3. False, it was called Maine Road.
4. True. 5. False, Gareth succeeded Sam Allardyce. 6. True.
7. False, Jordan began his career at Sunderland. 8. True.
9. False, he was signed from MK Dons. 10. True.

PAGE 46 · CLUB SEARCH

Huddersfield Town

PAGE 48 · WHICH BALL?

PAGE 49 · NAME THE SEASON

1. 2020/21. 2. 2012/13. 3. 1965/66. 4. 2021/22. 5. 2015/16.
6. 2020/21. 7. 2018/19. 8. 2011/12. 9. 2013/14. 10. 2008/09.

PAGE 52 · WHO ARE YER?

1. Taylor Harwood-Bellis. 2. Manuel Benson. 3. Adam Phillips.
4. Ashley Barnes. 5. Josh Brownhill. 6. Ian Maatsen.
7. Bailey Peacock-Farrell. 8. Jack Cork.

PAGE 60 · IDENTIFY THE STAR

1. Allison Becker. 2. Cristiano Ronaldo. 3. Philippe Coutinho.
4. Mikel Arteta. 5. Vinicius Junior. 6. Mark Noble. 7. Sergi Canos.
8. Ilkay Gundogan. 9. Ian Maatsen. 10. Nick Pope.